The Big Fight

The Big Fight

By Ethel and Leonard Kessler

Pictures by Pat Paris

GARRARD PUBLISHING COMPANY
CHAMPAIGN, ILLINOIS

For Chrissy Meyer

Library of Congress Cataloging in Publication Data

Kessler, Ethel.
    The big fight.

    SUMMARY: A friendship is tested when Pig accidentally
breaks Duck's new chair.
    [1. Ducks—Fiction. 2. Pigs—Fiction. 3. Friend-
ship—Fiction] I. Kessler, Leonard P., 1920-
joint author. II. Paris, Pat. III. Title.
PZ7.K483Bg   [E]   80-17244
ISBN 0-8116-7550-5

The Big Fight

"Hi, Duck,"
said Pig.
"Where is the
big surprise?"

"Here it is,"
said Duck.
"I made it."

"You made it!"
said Pig.
"What is it?"

"You should know,"
said Duck.
"It's a chair."

"A CHAIR?"
asked Pig.

9

"Sit on it,"
said Duck.

Pig sat down.

"Ouch!" yelled Pig.

11

"You broke my chair,"
said Duck.

"I hurt my foot,"
said Pig.

"You are big and fat,"
yelled Duck.

"You are a dumb duck,"
said Pig.
"I'm going home.
You are not my friend."

"You broke my chair.
You are not *my* friend,"
said Duck.

Duck was sad.
"Pig broke my chair.
I won't talk
to Pig again,"
said Duck.

"I won't talk
to Duck again,"
said Pig.

The next day

Duck went to the store.

She did not see Pig.

She went to the park.
She did not see Pig.

Duck asked Rabbit,
"Did you see Pig?"
"No," said Rabbit.

"Turtle,
did you see Pig?"
asked Duck.
"No, I haven't seen her,"
said Turtle.

"No one has seen Pig.
I think
she has hurt her foot,"
said Duck.
"Let's go to see her."

j38787

Turtle, Rabbit, and Duck
went to Pig's house.
"You knock on the door,"
said Turtle.
"Knock again," said Rabbit.

Pig came to the door.

"Hi, Duck.

Hi, Rabbit.

Hi, Turtle."

"We came to see you,"
said Duck.

"I'm glad you came,"
said Pig.
"Where have you been?"
asked Duck.

"I have been working,"
said Pig.
"I have made
a surprise for you.
Come in and see it."

"You made a chair for me!"
yelled Duck.

"Sit on it," said Pig.

"No, you sit on it,"
said Duck.

"Both of us
can sit on it,"
said Pig.

"Are you my friend?"
asked Pig.
"Yes," said Duck.
"We will always be friends."